POTATOES DON'T GROW ON TREES!

JEREMY AND JOSIE SCHROEDER

carrot

Carrots grow
in the ground.

pea

Peas grow
on vines.

potato

Top 5 countries

China
India
Russia
Ukraine
USA

Potatoes grow
in the ground.

Brussels sprout

Brussels sprouts
grow on stalks.

corn

Corn grows
on stalks.

asparagus

Asparagus grows
from the ground.

onion

Onions grow
in the ground.

cucumber

Cucumbers grow on vines.

mushroom

Mushrooms grow
on the ground.

lettuce

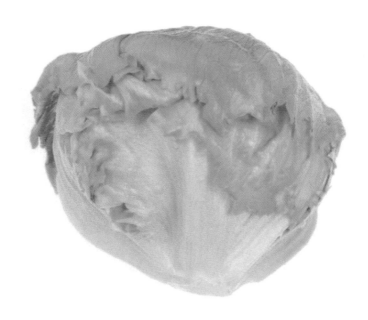

Lettuce grows
on the ground.

tomato

Top 5 countries

China
USA
Turkey
India
Egypt

Tomatoes grow
on plants.

broccoli

Top 5 countries

China
India
Spain
Italy
France

Broccoli grows
on plants.

pumpkin

Pumpkins
grow on vines
on the ground.

garlic

Top 5 countries

China
India
Korea
Russia
Egypt

Garlic grows
in the ground.

ISBN 978-91-88111-01-2

Hidden Toadstool Publishing; Linköping, Sweden; jeremy.josie.schroeder@gmail.com

Special thanks to Åsa Thor for design assistance.

Images and illustrations licensed from www.shutterstock.com

Front/Back cover
text- VOOK
tree- Matthew Cole
potato- pichayasri
farmer- Teguh Mujiono
clouds- Teguh Mujiono
sack- Matthew Cole
grass- hehehe

Title page
text- VOOK
tree- Matthew Cole
potato- pichayasri
sack- Matthew Cole

Legend for images

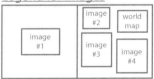

World map
Serban Bogdan

Carrot
image #1- LorenzoArcobasso
image #2- Peter Zijlstra
image #3- Sergey Goruppa
image #4- Martin Nemec

Pea
image #1- ravl
image #2- LU HUANFENG
image #3- Nadezhda Nesterova
image #4- Ruud Morijn Photographer

Potato
image #1- Africa Studio
image #2- Deep OV
image #3- Madlen
image #4- Ramon grosso dolarea

Brussels sprout
image #1- Gtranquillity
image #2- Peter Zijlstra
image #3- Winning7799
image #4- CroMary

Corn
image #1- Neamov
image #2- Maks Narodenko
image #3- Fedor Selivanov
image #4- Labrynthe

Asparagus
image #1- Hong Vo
image #2- Anna Breitenberger
image #3- elena moiseeva
image #4- LianeM

Onion
image #1- Nattika
image #2- EM Arts
image #3- FotograFFF
image #4- Straight 8 Photography

Cucumber
image #1- Anna Sedneva
image #2- Alexey Laputin
image #3- Nadezhda Nesterova
image #4- Offscreen

Mushroom
image #1- Nattika
image #2- turtix
image #3- Kuttelvaserova Stuchelova
image #4- Piotr Marcinski

Lettuce
image #1- Dafinka
image #2- Swapan Photography
image #3- pedrolieb
image #4- Kuttelvaserova Stuchelova

Tomato
image #1- Africa Studio
image #2- Vitaly Korovin
image #3- Swetlana Wall
image #4- luigi nifosi

Broccoli
image #1- pilipphoto
image #2- phasinphoto
image #3- ChameleonsEye
image #4- Jim Parkin

Pumpkin
image #1- Bozena Fulawka
image #2- wiktord
image #3- MNStudio
image #4- Marilyn Volan

Garlic
image #1- Maks Narodenko
image #2- Madlen
image #3- Denis and Yulia Pogostins
image #4- yuris

Made in the USA
Middletown, DE
02 October 2020